Stories of Regional America—some humorous, some filled with pathos—spotlight both the likes and differences of special peoples in colorful places. These peoples form the melting pot, which has become America. The action-filled accounts, each based on true fact, give the reader a deeper appreciation of his cultural background and a greater understanding of the peoples who have made his heritage possible.

CAMELS
Are Meaner Than Mules

BY MARY CALHOUN

ILLUSTRATED BY HERMAN B. VESTAL

GARRARD PUBLISHING COMPANY
CHAMPAIGN, ILLINOIS

Contents

1. Gertie the Mean-Mouthed Monster

That camel looked me straight in the eye. I looked her straight back. I tried a new voice.

"Please, Gertie," I said, sweet as molasses, "you slog-footed humpbacked, miserable, ugly beast—please, let me catch you!"

Gertie only tossed her head, looked off into the middle part of nowhere, and chewed her cud.

There I was, Pete the mule driver—and one of the army's best, if I do say so myself—out on the Texas prairie at midnight, trying to catch a camel. And there she stood on those skinny stilt-legs, holding that little head way up in the air.

Her head at the end of her snake-neck was nothing but big eyes and squashed-together snoot. I don't know how she managed to look so proud.

I jumped for her bridle again. "Get that smart-aleck neck down here!" I said.

She just wove her neck around and looked down her snoot at me like a queen. Then she worked those rubbery lips, opened her mouth, and spit.

But I knew her tricks and dodged. "Mean-mouthed monster! I'll outsmart you yet!"

It was her fault we were out there. It was Gertie's idea to run off and play after a hard day's 25-mile march. She don't care if I had to go out and track her down. Camels are meaner than mules any day or night, I'll tell you!

Or maybe it was Jefferson Davis' fault, for the camel experiment was his fancy idea in the first place. Somewhere he got the notion that camels would make good pack animals in the Southwest Territory. He had 34 of 'em shipped over from Egypt and Turkey, some of those

foreign outlandish kind of places that *would* pro-
duce a thing like a camel.

That was back in the days before the Civil
War. Old Davis same as said, "All right, army,
here's you a new-type pack-mule. Try this bunch
out in *our* desert." Then he went back to his
job with the War Department in Washington
and left us mule skinners to turn into camel
drivers the best way we could.

Yessir, I was on that first camel trip through
the American desert, back in 1857, led by
Lieutenant Edward F. Beale. We started out from
Camp Val Verde, Texas, and surveyed a new
emigrant route between Fort Defiance, New
Mexico, and the Colorado River. Before we
ended up, we'd gone clear to California with
those beasts.

I guess we made quite a sight, heading out
through southwest Texas for the Rio Grande.
There was the train of supply wagons and mules
and men on horses. Then after it came a long
string of loop-necked camels, humping along
against the horizon, big pack-loads of supplies
on their backs. Not all of my mule skinner pals

stuck it out to California, though. Some men deserted, rather than work with those miserable camels.

You want to know what it was like, hustling a flock of camels around the American desert? I'll tell you. It was like working with an invention of the devil! Camels! They look as if the devil had tried his hand at creating an animal and turned out a critter that looked like a mistake going in six directions. The devil must have said, "Oh, well, pshaw! Act like the devil then, too!"

Let me put it this way: a camel is a bad-tempered, complaining, stupid, smelly grouch.

True, mules can be mean. When you try to load 'em up, there's all that kicking-and-biting-and-heehawing hoorah. But then a mule will settle down to a good day's carrying work, and a mule's a pretty good pardner for a man on a march.

But camels! They are another type of four-legged beast, entire. I found that out when first I reported to Val Verde, all curious to see what a camel looked like. Tall and ugly, with those humps, I thought. But about like a mule, I thought, when I saw the fellows trying to load up. They were yelling at the beasts and hitting their knees with sticks to make them kneel, to get the packs on their backs. I soon found out that camels don't resemble mules any more than a snake resembles a hoot owl. And you can bet camels are meaner than mules.

Humpbacked trouble, that's what us mule drivers found, when we started out that trip. If a camel isn't trying to kick you at loading time, he's trying to bite. If not bite, then spit. And complain? Pshaw, you never heard a woman complain like a camel can. He starts groaning the minute he sees you coming with the pack, argues just the same when you take it off. And *all* the trip, *every* step, mutter and grumble, complaining and smelling all the way.

Smell? Why, a pack of coyotes on a hill two miles away would stampede when they caught a whiff of camel. As for the horses, they were in a nervous furor half the time from the camels' foreign smell.

Then with all that meanness and smell all day

long, what do they do at night? Run off. They're not tired. Oh, no, now it's camel playtime, tra la!

That was the thing about the camels that made us mule drivers the maddest. There we'd be, worn out and disgusted from herding camels across 25 miles of hot prairie. We'd get all bedded down, and "Camel missing!" somebody would shout. Then it was up from the bedroll and out on a horse on a camel chase.

That's what I was doing when I caught up with that main troublemaker, Gertie. Gertie—I called her that after the meanest, stubbornest, old woman in my hometown. Gertie was the leader of the camels in my charge, and sometimes she took her pals a-gallivanting with her. But that night she was alone, queening around in the moonlight, trying to spit me in the eye.

I was fit to be tied, I was so mad, but I tried again. I got around on her side and reached up, slowlike, for her bridle. She jerked her neck away and danced off on those big, splay feet. "Ha ha, you can't catch me!" Games, she wants to play, in the middle of the night!

I followed her, stumbling over the rocks in my boots, for I'd left my horse over by a mesquite bush. The horse bucked so at Gertie's smell, it was no help at catching a fidgety camel. Then Gertie spotted a tasty clump of greasewood weeds, bent her neck down to nibble at it, and I snatched her bridle.

"Got you!"

"N-nnwhrr," she groaned.

But she stumped along behind, with no more spitting or biting. Game-time was over. I got her back to the horse, tied my saddle rope to her bridle, and started for camp, five miles or so away.

It wasn't no pleasure trip. They call camels "ships of the desert." Huh! Bringing Gertie in was more like towing a balky rowboat in a cross current. First she strayed off to the side after a snack of cactus, nearly jerking the saddle out from under me. Next she tramped up on the horse's heels, breathing her foul breath all over us and making the horse skittish.

I looked back at that pinhead sailing in the air behind me. I said to myself, "Pete, you look

at the size of that camel's head, and you *know* there can't be many brains in there. You *got* to be smarter'n that camel!"

I looked at Gertie's head again, and you know what her face looked like? Contented. She'd had her fun. Well, sir, no animal as dumb-looking as a camel is going to outsmart me. I'm from Missouri, and I can out-stubborn a camel any day.

Right then and there in the moonlight I vowed, "Gertie, you monster, this is the last night you run off!"

2. Pete the Showman

Next day Gertie grinned at me. I swear she did! When I was loading on her pack, she turned her head to watch me, pulled back her lips and grinned. It was as if to say, "Make all the vows you want, you bowlegged farmboy from Missouri. I'll run off any night I feel like it!"

Huh! I thought. I'll make you grin out of the other side of your mouth, you rubbernecked stack of bones!

I didn't care whether the great camel experiment was a success. I hoped to the high hills it *wasn't* a success, if it meant I had to be a camel driver for the rest of my tour of duty

with the army. No, sir, this battle was strictly between me and Gertie.

As I rode alongside the camel train, I turned over the problem. Nothing seemed to stop camels when they took a notion to wander. I had staked Gertie to the ground. She just leaned and leaned until she'd pulled up the stake. I had hobbled her. She just chewed through the rope. Camels have got a mean bite—with those big yellow teeth—let me tell you.

I glared at Gertie, swaying along there, carrying her pack, fresh as a daisy after her night's outing. I wasn't surprised. At the end of a day's march, the camels started resting the minute they stopped walking. By the time we'd made camp, cooked supper, eaten it, and were ready to turn in for the night, the camels were done with their naps. They were ready for another 25-mile jaunt. We'd already found out how strong they were. Those camels padded along on cushion-toed feet in the sand, and they could carry 500-pound loads, twice as much as a mule could heft. They could eat anything, and especially loved stickery weeds. They could go

19

for days on the moisture in a cactus. So, for certain, camels must get along on less rest than any other animal needs.

Therefore, I figured, the thing to do was to wear out Gertie again last thing before I slept. Only—how, when I was worn out myself?

Then along about mid-afternoon, time to camp, we rode up to the answer. It was a Mexican village.

Clustered around a spring were a few adobe houses and sod shacks. There were even some green willows near the spring and vegetable gardens in between the houses, the first real greenery we'd seen for days. That's what a little water will do for this bare-dirt country. Maybe southwest Texas doesn't have sand like the Sahara Desert, but it's surely covered with sandy dirt. The village was a lively spot, though, with kids and dogs all over the place. The wide-eyed kids ran out to see the camels, but the dogs took one sniff and ran ki-yii-ing off with their tails between their legs. Women in shawls came to the doorways, and the men shoved back their hats to take a look. We were a sensation.

Lieutenant Beale started to ride on by, for he never pitched camp near settlements. But I looked at those big-eyed children, and I began to get an idea. I rode up to the lieutenant and talked fast. I persuaded him to camp just over the hill.

Now you got to understand that Lieutenant Beale thought those camels were just about perfect. Called 'em "noble beasts," and always talked about how patient and strong they were. But he knew they ran off at night, so he agreed to try my plan for the sake of smoothing out the last little bit of imperfection in his precious camels.

After supper we took Gertie and her best playmate and rode them over to the village. My idea was that all those kids would want to ride a camel, and after that the beasts would be too tired to run off. I was right about one thing, the kids went for the camels.

When we came clumping between the houses, the doorways filled with people. Little girls peeked around their mothers' skirts. We got off the camels, and one of the men came out.

He said, "You the showman? You gotta lotta camelos?" The Mexican was plenty curious, but he was keeping a safe distance from the camels.

"Yes," I said, "and monkeys and—"

Beale cut the foolery short. "You want to ride a camel?"

"No, no!" The man backed off. "Gotta sore leg, see?" He made a show of limping and groaning.

However, a crowd of boys had gathered, and one of them popped forward, tapping his chest. "Me, me!"

"All right, Buster, come right over here. Kneel," I told Gertie. "Nn-oo-whrr," she balked, like always. I whacked her knees with my stick, and she folded down, muttering. I showed the boy how to mount her. "Hook one leg around this thing on the saddle," I said. Then I gave him the reins, and said, "Hang on!"

Gertie wove her head around and stared at the boy while she chewed. She had a thoughtful look on her face, like she might be about to spit. I smacked her knees again.

"Goom! Rise!" I shouted.

Whereupon Gertie started floundering up, camel-fashion. First she rose to her foreknees, pitching the boy backwards. Then up came her hind legs, all the way, and the boy flopped frontways on her neck. Then she straightened up her front legs, and he tipped backwards again. The poor kid's face was a scared gray, but he held tight to the reins with one hand and the saddle post with the other. His pals were watching. It was a test of his manhood.

"Yaayy!" all the kids yelled when the boy and camel were upright.

I led Gertie out. The boy had more news coming, because a camel picks up one foot at a time. Gertie began walking, and the kid began jolting in four directions. Still, he was game. He even grinned and let go of the post to wave at his friends. I started running with Gertie, and she broke into a trot. Now the kid was *swaying* four ways at once. He kept smiling, but his face

looked green around the edges, so I brought Gertie back to the crowd and made her kneel.

"Next?"

The boy tumbled off, laughing and talking a streak, and all the Mexicans began chattering like a gang of magpies. Now every boy had to prove his manhood. Lieutenant Beale took one youngster on his camel, and I took another. But my boy was so excited he was whooped up to a fare-thee-well.

"Faster, faster!" he yelled, pounding Gertie's side with his leg.

Gertie broke into a trot and like to run over me. I jumped out of the way and lost hold of her bridle.

Well, I sort of hate to tell what happened next. Beale took it out of my pay. Gertie went clopping through a vegetable patch, knocking over bean bushes and stomping down corn. She was on a running rampage, but she didn't know where to go in all that greenery. Next she came tearing back through another patch, dragging bean poles with her. Finally she went roaring into a third garden, tipped off the boy, and began eating the hot peppers on the vines. Those vegetable patches looked as if a cyclone had hit them.

The Mexicans weren't very happy that night. Beale had to pay them off in bacon slabs before they'd quit hollering and swarming up to our camp, shaking sticks at us.

I wasn't happy that night, either. Because about midnight Gertie ran off, same as ever. After I'd found her and brought her back, I was kind of surprised at my powers of imagination. I'd thought up many new names to call that camel.

3. The Miserable Fourth of July

When we loaded up for the march next morning I took a lot of razzing from the fellows. All the boys had to make smart-aleck remarks like, "Hey, Pete, Gertie's still grinning!" And, "What's become of the old know-how, Pete? Thought the best mule skinner in the army could outsmart a camel." And, "Say, boys! Look what Gertie's got tied to her apron strings!"

By now everybody on the expedition knew about my feud with Gertie. Plenty of the other mule drivers had to chase camels down in the night, so they all were rooting for me to solve the problem. But nobody was taking any bets on me, I could see that. Everybody was laughing at me. Then I looked at Gertie, and, by tunket, she was laughing at me, too! Anyway, she had her lips pulled back, and she was either laughing or fixing to spit at me through her teeth.

"By the everlasting!" I yelled. "I'll wear you out today, you—"

I heaved up a big rock and crammed it into Gertie's pack. I was hauling at another boulder, when Lieutenant Beale rode up.

"Fixing to move some countryside, Pete?" he asked, mild as pudding. "For your information, I've been told that a camel can carry a 1000-pound load without tiring. That's a lot of rocks."

"Ha ha ha!" Oh, yes, everybody had a good time laughing at old Pete.

"Pshaw!" I said. I slammed my hat on my head and stamped away to saddle my horse.

It was a worthless day, too. At the end of it Gertie ran away again. Bringing her back to camp, I got to thinking about how many more miles it was to California. At this rate, time we got there, I'd have traveled twice the distance, just tracking down Gertie at night.

30

The next day was July 4, and it was the most miserable Fourth of July I have spent in my life. It rained. Talk about rain! It was like we were underneath an ocean bed, and somebody pulled the plug. For days we'd been crossing hot, dry prairie. Then that day, when the three a.m. bugle roused us, there it was raining torrents. Have you ever tried to load camels and harness mules to wagons in the dark, in pouring down rain? It wasn't just me—all the men were using colorful words not heard before, ones they'd been saving up for a particularly interesting occasion.

The Glorious Fourth went from disagreeable to worse. Of course, there was no coffee or breakfast, because it was impossible to raise a fire in the rain. So we rode along, hour after hour in the rain—hungry, soaking wet, and mad. It was slow going, for the wagons, loaded heavy with supplies, kept sticking in the mud. The sandy dirt had turned to thick, gooey clay. Also there was a gusty wind that kept slapping cold, miserable rain in my face. I never thought I'd live to see the day I'd be so wet in desert country.

I wondered what the camels thought of the rain, wondered if they'd ever been rained on. I looked at Gertie, hoping she was at least half as miserable as I was. If she was, I couldn't tell it. She just plodded along, one foot after another, with a dreamy look on her snoot. Once in a while she blinked at the water sliding down her long eyelashes.

Naturally, when everything was all wet and muddy, we had to come to some hills. The mules were really working to haul the wagons uphill, with the clay clogging the wheels. On the second hill the lead wagon stopped, and all the mule skinners could crack their whips till Kingdom come. The wagon wheels were stuck fast in the mud, and the mule team couldn't pull the lead wagon out. One of the drivers started to unhitch another mule team to take forward to help the lead team, when I got an idea.

"Hey!" I called out. "Don't bother unhitching that team. Remember the noble beasts! That strong, powerful Nonesuch—the camel! Try Gertie, here."

33

Lieutenant Beale rode up on his horse, and he looked interested. "I doubt it'll work, Pete, but it's worth the experiment, just to find out whether a camel can outhaul two mules."

I got off my horse and led Gertie forward, pack-load on her back. I had a hard time slogging through the mud in my boots, but she just squooshed along on her big flat feet. At the lead wagon we took the mules out of the traces, and I hitched the harness around Gertie as best I could.

Mainly camels are carrying beasts, carrying packs or people on their humps. However, Lieutenant Beale said he'd been told that a camel, when hitched to a wagon, can pull up to 1600 pounds.

Gertie didn't think so. "Nn-whrrr!" she whined. She wove her gooseneck around to look at the monstrous thing she was hitched up to, rolled her popeyes, and spit. "Groan!" she said. What a horrible thing to happen to a nice lady camel!

"Goom! Move! Let's go!" I yelled, pulling her bridle and slipping around in the mud. "Come on Gertie, move!"

"Forget it, Pete," said Lieutenant Beale. "She doesn't know what to do."

No, sir, I wasn't going to forget it. If I could get Gertie to haul wagons out of the mud, while carrying a 500-pound pack on her back, maybe *tonight* she'd be too tired to run off!

I snatched up a branch of greasewood and held it out in front of her nose.

"Here it is, Gertie, food! Come and get it."

She leaned forward, and I kept moving the greasewood back, like a carrot in front of a donkey.

"Come on, Gertie, that's the girl." I scratched her ears but held the weeds out of reach. "Pull, Gertie," I pleaded, scratching away behind her ears. "You can do it now—pull!"

And she did. Gertie strained ahead toward the greasewood. She couldn't reach it. She hea-av-ved forward.

I kept scratching Gertie's ears and holding the weeds at arm's length.

Squ-ush, the wagon wheels began to move. Gertie put her shoulders into the job. The wagon wheels rolled free. Gertie kept going, and she hauled that wagon right up the hill!—Yes, I did give her the greasewood.

"Hurrah!" shouted Beale. "Hurrah for the camels! Hurrah for Gertie!"

Ha ha! I thought.

Sure enough, every time a wagon got stuck in the plowed-up mud on the hill, Gertie and some of the other camels were hitched up to pull it out.

That ought to tire out the old girl, I thought.

"Heh heh, old Pete's not so dumb," I told the fellows.

Well, we got all the wagons hauled over that hill and down the other side, but the next hill was the end. Dead Man's Pass, they call it. It was the steepest rise yet. Camels and mules were heaving away in the mud and rain, and we were nearly to the top when a wagon tongue broke. There was no chance of going any further until we found a piece of timber for a new wagon tongue.

38

So there we camped, on the side of Dead Man's Pass, in the rain and the mud—with no stream or water hole for the animals to drink from. Somebody surely was having a fine Fourth of July joke on this camel expedition.

After a while, though, the rain drizzled out and stopped, and finally the cook managed to get a campfire going. He started coffee made with rainwater, and pretty soon there were some encouraging smells in the air on Dead Man's Pass —the smells of coffee boiling and stew bubbling in the pot. Some of the fellows got to laughing, and everybody cheered up considerably. I began to feel downright happy. Tonight I'd sleep sound.

I glanced over at the camels and saw Gertie folded down on her knees, having a good snooze. She'd had enough workout today to kill five mules.

"Sleep tight, Gertie," I said. "Don't wake till morning light!"

After a good bellyful of stew I stretched out in my bedroll like I was going to sleep for ten years, I was so tired. It didn't seem like ten minutes until somebody was shaking me.

"Camel missing," said the fellow on watch duty. "I understand her name is Gertie."

"And my name is a sad son of a sea cook!" I came roaring out of my sack. "I'll kill her! I'll kill her!"

I found Gertie down at the bottom of the pass, happily stomping around in a gully, where she'd found water. When I came along she lifted her head from drinking, pulled her lips back and blew bubbles. I strongly considered thrashing her with a cactus.

However, punishment wouldn't faze a camel tough enough to haul a 500-pound pack-load *and* wagons all day in the mud.

No, tired as I was, I still understood the situation clear enough. The only way to keep Gertie in camp at night was to make her *want* to stay there. How? Well, I'd work on that one again tomorrow. I'd had enough for one Fourth of July.

All in all, it was the kind of day that made me wish I'd followed my original intention as a boy and run away to sea.

4. Camel Races

Maybe it was all that rain had soaked into my head and washed my brains clean. Or maybe it was desperation. Anyway, next morning I woke up with an IDEA. I came leaping out of my bed-roll like a boy on Christmas morning and went to find Lieutenant Beale.

I found him by the cookfire, getting his first coffee into him.

Sly as a possum in a pawpaw patch, I said, "Very enduring beast, the camel."

"You're right there, Pete," says he, smiling. "I'm beginning to think there isn't anything a camel can't do."

"Except stay put at night," says I.

The lieutenant quit smiling. He didn't like to be reminded of the trouble the camels gave. He was sure that camels were going to be the greatest aid yet in opening up emigrant routes to the western territories.

So then I told him my plan. Camel races, that's what I had in mind. Camels liked to go for a run at night. All right, let 'em run, get it out of their systems. Then maybe they'd stay put, tired out and content, when we wanted to sleep. Besides, some of our beasts were dromedaries, racing camels, and some of them had been running away, too. Gertie was just a plain pack camel, but she'd shown pretty good steam in those Mexican vegetable gardens.

"Let's see whether dromedaries really can run faster than camels," I said.

Beale bit on that one. He was always hot on experimenting with his noble beasts.

"All right," he said, "but there'd better not be any trouble. I hold you responsible, Pete."

There wasn't any trouble, either. Not what you'd really call trouble.

That night after supper we picked out our racers. I rode Gertie, and Lieutenant Beale and another fellow rode dromedaries. We chose a pile of rocks a mile or so out for the turning point. The men crowded around while we lined up at the starting mark. "Ready, get set, go!" they shouted.

I toed Gertie, and she started walking. So did the dromedaries. But we kicked them and yelled, and they stepped along faster until they broke into a trot. I could hear the men hollering like at a horse race, rooting for their favorites. "Come on, Mohamet!" "Get up there, Seid!" Not many were yelling for Gertie, for they didn't expect much of a pack camel.

At first I didn't care whether we won or not. I just wanted to give those pesky beasts a good tiring run. But Gertie kept clumping along at a good pace, right up alongside the dromedaries, and I guess I got carried away with excitement.

I started shouting, "That's it, Gertie! Keep going!" We were nose and nose with the dromedaries. Then we pulled out ahead of them both. "Come on, camel! Show your steam!"

We rounded the rocks and came pounding back. And what do you know? Gertie won.

"Good girl, Gertie!" I patted her head and scratched her ears, just as if I liked her. Carried away, like I say.

The men were "hip-hipping" and laughing, but Lieutenant Beale didn't look pleased. I knew he had the picture that dromedaries were swift beasts to carry soldiers after Indian raiders and on scouting parties. And the dromedaries were fast, too. Only Gertie was faster. Maybe those nightly jaunts kept her legs in good shape. Anyway, I should have stopped right there, with Beale looking so put out, but I was all excited.

I said, "How about matching a camel with a horse, Lieutenant? How about a test?"

You only had to say "test" to him. He got his favorite horse, a powerful gray, though he said it wouldn't be fair, because the camels must be winded by now. Still, they were famed for their endurance. So, to make it a real test, he picked a fresh dromedary for the other rider and let me ride Gertie again, to see how strong she really was.

46

"Ready, get set, go!"

The horse was off like a shot, of course, but Gertie and the dromedary ambled away from the mark. Soon I got Gertie to trotting, and the dromedary trotted for the other fellow. Before we got to the rocks Beale passed us going back, waving his hat. However, knowing the horse would get a head start, we'd set the race to be three times out to the rocks and back. Gertie and I kept galloping, camel-style. We were ahead of the dromedary, and Gertie wasn't even breathing hard. I vow, that camel liked to run.

"Come on, Gertie, good old camel!" I kept yelling. "We're gaining. Now we're gaining. You can do it, Gertie!" I'd forgotten everything else, so possessed was I to catch up with that horse's tail.

It was the third time around the rocks, and Beale's gray was beginning to flag. But Gertie kept loping along like running forever was her natural state. Now we were on our way back, we'd passed the dromedary going the other direction. Gertie was pulling up to the gray's tail, up along its flank. "Win, Gertie, win!" I was hollering—and now we were nose and nose with the horse. And ahead!

"Sweet old girl! Keep going!" I panted.

We were in the lead. The men were cheering. We were about to win! Suddenly I realized I didn't hear hoofbeats behind us, and I looked back. Beale's horse had stumbled and thrown him to the ground.

It's to my shame to admit it. I galloped Gertie right on to the finish line, to beat that drome-

dary, too. Beale came limping in last with the horse, said it had stumbled on an outcropping of rock. So I won the camel-dromedary-horse race.

But I didn't really win. Not at what I'd set out to do. Gertie ran away that night, along with a racing dromedary. It was as if the race had just whetted their appetites. When I caught up with them, Gertie looked down at me from her queen-neck, her face as contented as ever.

It's a bitter thing for a man my age to admit he's been defeated by a stupid camel. The fellows knew better than to talk to me the next day.

On that day's march Lieutenant Beale was very glum. He was too true a man to outright blame me for laming his good horse, but I knew enough not to suggest any more plans to him on this expedition. It didn't matter. I'd given up. I was mad and discouraged—and sore in the seat from jouncing on Gertie in the races.

When we stopped, all I could do was sink down by the campfire and ache. The cook rubbed some stuff on me, and after supper I felt more comfortable. Looking at the sunset, I started in to singing, slow and easy, songs about home and faraway sweethearts. Some of the fellows around the fire joined in, and one with a harmonica whiffled on it, sweet and sad. Even the camels shuffled closer and listened, blinking their eyes. In the end a pleasant evening was had by all.

In fact, a pleasant night was had by all, for none of the camels strayed off.

Oho, I congratulated myself next morning, you

were right, Pete! You got those loose-footed camels tired out at racing, all right. It just took the next day's march for them to know it!

That night I padded my seat and rode Gertie three times out to the cliffs. She made it in quick time, so I could turn in early.

"Good night, Gertie, old monster," I said, scratching her ears when I climbed off. I'd won, I could afford to be generous to a poor dumb beast. "Sleep tight!"

Huh. Along about midnight I woke up, looked around, and—that's right, Gertie was gone. When I finally tracked her down out by the cliffs, there she was with two other camels. Three old ladies galumphing around in the moonlight, having themselves an outing.

"Think you've beat me?" I said bitterly. "Well,
you have!"

After I got the camels rounded up and roped
to my saddle, I wouldn't spare them a look on
the way back. Not even when Gertie came nosing
up to me with her stinking breath. Monsters, all
of them!

5. Lullaby for Camels

You never saw a sadder man than I was, at the end of the next day's march. The best mule skinner in the army, defeated by a camel. I'd never be able to hold my head up again—if I lived through the trip, chasing Gertie down every night.

At least, that night I didn't have to run after strays. It was my turn for watch-duty on the late shift—eleven p.m. until rising. I slept early and got up tired. I made the rounds of the camp, saw Gertie and her pals were browsing on some greasewood, and settled myself by the campfire. I nearly nodded off to sleep again, looking at the red coals, so I started singing to keep myself awake. The camels were hobbled to graze, and pretty soon Gertie and two friends shuffled over near the fire.

"Go on away from me," I muttered, throwing a dirt clod at them.

They trundled off, and I began humming and singing again, soft, so as not to wake the men. But as soon as I started, Gertie began to edge closer, so I shut up the singing. After a time I noticed she was grazing too far out from camp.

"Come back here!" I called, but she kept walking in the other direction. I knew as soon as she got out of sight she'd chew loose her hobble rope. I was about to raise the shout that a camel was going off, when I got an idea.

I started singing, "My faraway Rose, a-waiting for me." Sure enough, Gertie stopped. She swung her head around and started back.

What do you know! It worked! A song was like a rope on her neck.

I tested it out then. I quit singing, and soon Gertie and some other camels began to stray out of bounds. I sang loud, and here they all came

back. They crowded in close and stood there looking at me with their big wet eyes while I hummed soft. Gertie's head swayed on her neck as she chewed her cud and listened to me sing through my nose. Once she belched and blinked her eyes in apology as her lump of cud traveled down her neck. Mustn't interrupt the music. Oh, no. I was the prettiest thing those camels ever did hear.

Well, sir, that's what I did all night. Every time Gertie or the others moved too far away, I sang something, and they'd come back. A few years later I was told that's how the Arab drivers get their camels to travel at night, singing to them in a kind of minor wail. Luckily I found the trick all by myself.

Lieutenant Beale was as happy as a horse with sugar when I told him next day. Now the last little problem with his darling camels was solved. It was, too, so far as their straying went. After that, whoever was on watch sang to them, and it was seldom that a camel ever ran off. They were especially fond of listening to the man with the harmonica.

As for Gertie, that's a slightly different story. The morning after my first camel-concert I was bragging to the fellows while I put the pack on Gertie.

"I outsmarted her, all right!" I said. "I told myself I had more brains than a pinheaded camel. Now I know how to control her," I ran on.

Then I noticed the fellows were laughing. "Outsmart, nothing!" said one. "She loves you!"

"Ahhh!" I cried.

For Gertie was leaning her head on my shoulder, blinking those big eyes as if she adored me and drooling green saliva down my jacket. She was turning her ears for me to scratch them.

That's the way it went for the rest of the trip. Gertie followed me around like a pet lapdog and drooled on me every chance she got. No, she wouldn't run off anymore. Now I couldn't get rid of her!

Oh, she still grumbled and stank. But she

never tried to bite me or spit at me again. She even got so she'd kneel when I barely rubbed her knees with the stick. All she wanted was for me to scratch her ears now and then, give her a little kindness, and sing her a bedtime song. And you know, I'll have to admit it. By the end of the trip I'd come to respect Gertie and her friends. I'd seen them work. They were good, enduring beasts in the desert.

Yes, the camel experiment was a success. The camels proved their worth in the Southwest. They lived on weeds and very little water. They carried their 500-pound loads, and they walked strong all the way to California. After that, the army did work the animals a few times on mail routes and road surveying. It was too bad the Civil War broke out and distracted the government from doing anything more with the camels.

When we got into war, the camels were dumped, put up for auction. Lieutenant Beale bought a few, and took 'em up to his ranch in the California mountains. I heard tell it was quite a sight when he drove to Los Angeles in a carriage hitched to a team of dromedaries.

But I don't go in for any of that fancy foolishness. Gertie, here, is a working animal. Yes, when they put her up on the auction block, I bought her. What are you going to do, when a camel's in love with you?

Besides, she makes a good pardner at working this mining claim, carrying ore. And I'm used to riding a camel now. The way she travels over the sand, I'd never have a mule again. She may be ugly and smelly and grumpier than any grouch, but Gertie will work till the day she drops. And you got to respect a camel for that.

MEET THE AUTHOR

MARY CALHOUN was born and raised along the banks of the Mississippi River. She studied journalism at the University of Iowa and worked as a newspaper reporter for several years before starting to write books. Two young sons, Mike and Greg, urged her to make up stories for them, and writing the tales down for other children to enjoy was a natural step. Mrs. Calhoun, whose work ranges from picture books to teenage novels, now lives in a small town in western Colorado where she enjoys rambling in the hills and woods. Folklore remains her special interest, and through extensive research she has captured the speech, mannerisms, and the ways of the people she writes about.

MEET THE ARTIST

HERMAN B. VESTAL loves both painting and the sea. Before studying art at the National Academy of Design and Pratt Institute, he went to sea in the Merchant Marine. During World War II he served in the Coast Guard as a combat artist. His assignments included recording the Normandy landing and the invasion of Iwo Jima. Today, his interest in the sea continues through his hobby — sailboat racing. Primarily a book illustrator, Mr. Vestal also enjoys doing watercolors and is a member of the American Watercolor Society. Mr. Vestal, his wife, and son live in Little Silver, New Jersey.